leapf

D0374186

Freddie's Fears

First published in 2001 by
Franklin Watts
96 Leonard Street
London
EC2A 4XD

Franklin Watts Australia
56 O'Riordan Street
Alexandria
NSW 2015

A CIP catalogue record for this book is available
from the British Library.

ISBN 0 7496 3929 6 (hbk)
ISBN 0 7496 4382 X (pbk)

Series Editor: Louise John
Series Advisor: Dr Barrie Wade
Series Designer: Jason Anscomb

Printed in Hong Kong

For Freddie – HR

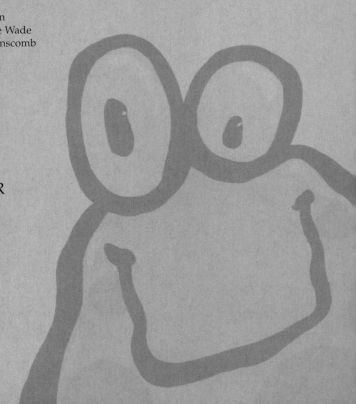

Freddie's Fears

by Hilary Robinson

Illustrated by Ross Collins

W
FRANKLIN WATTS
LONDON·SYDNEY

Freddie was frightened of frogs.

He was scared stiff of
spiders.

And he didn't like dogs.

Newts made him nervous.

He was worried by worms.

He thought that all gerbils were covered in germs.

Mice were a menace.

And snakes made him scream.

He feared all the flies that licked his ice-cream.

Then one day his daddy
said all of his fears
were just in his head.

"Freddie, you know,
all of these fears
will just have to go."

"Now, take a deep breath and why don't you let ...

... each of the animals
become a real pet?"

Now frogs are his friends.

And spiders are special.

Dogs don't alarm him.

And all the newts nestle
behind his big bed ...

... where the snakes and
the flies are really well fed.

He tells all of his friends
nothing gives him a fright ...

... except for the things that go bump in the night!

Leapfrog has been specially designed to fit the requirements of the National Literacy Strategy. It offers real books for beginning readers by top authors and illustrators.

There are 25 Leapfrog stories to choose from:

The Bossy Cockerel

Written by Margaret Nash,
illustrated by Elisabeth Moseng

Bill's Baggy Trousers

Written by Susan Gates,
illustrated by Anni Axworthy

Mr Spotty's Potty

Written by Hilary Robinson,
illustrated by Peter Utton

Little Joe's Big Race

Written by Andy Blackford,
illustrated by Tim Archbold

The Little Star

Written by Deborah Nash,
illustrated by Richard Morgan

The Cheeky Monkey

Written by Anne Cassidy,
illustrated by Lisa Smith

Selfish Sophie

Written by Damian Kelleher,
illustrated by Georgie Birkett

Recycled!

Written by Jillian Powell,
illustrated by Amanda Wood

Felix on the Move

Written by Maeve Friel,
illustrated by Beccy Blake

Pippa and Poppa

Written by Anne Cassidy,
illustrated by Philip Norman

Jack's Party

Written by Ann Bryant,
illustrated by Claire Henley

The Best Snowman

Written by Margaret Nash,
illustrated by Jörg Saupe

Eight Enormous Elephants

Written by Penny Dolan,
illustrated by Leo Broadley

Mary and the Fairy

Written by Penny Dolan,
illustrated by Deborah Allwright

The Crying Princess

Written by Anne Cassidy,
illustrated by Colin Paine

Cinderella

Written by Barrie Wade,
illustrated by Julie Monks

The Three Little Pigs

Written by Maggie Moore,
illustrated by Rob Hefferan

The Three Billy Goats Gruff

Written by Barrie Wade,
illustrated by Nicola Evans

Goldilocks and the Three Bears

Written by Barrie Wade,
illustrated by Kristina Stephenson

Jack and the Beanstalk

Written by Maggie Moore,
illustrated by Steve Cox

Little Red Riding Hood

Written by Maggie Moore,
illustrated by Paula Knight

Jasper and Jess

Written by Anne Cassidy,
illustrated by François Hall

The Lazy Scarecrow

Written by Jillian Powell,
illustrated by Jayne Coughlin

The Naughty Puppy

Written by Jillian Powell,
illustrated by Summer Durantz

Freddie's Fears

Written by Hilary Robinson,
illustrated by Ross Collins